To all the grandmothers and grandfathers
who make us better people with their stories.

To Fidela, Quinai, Felipa, Pedro, Isabel, Paco, Teresa, Eduardo, Sara, Miguel, Soco,
Vicente, Rosita, Mariano, Ter, Lorenzo, Cuki, Manolo, Inma, Luis, Paca, Félix,
Herminia, Mercedes, Concha, Candelas, Fernando, Pilar, Pepe, Olga, Antonio, Merce,
Pedro, Pilipo, Julio, Pilipi, Maruja, Ángel, Russer, Benjamin, Isbi, Momo, Maira, Dioni,
Azu, Chema, Vicky, Gerardo, Chusa, José Miguel, Almu, Ángel, Mª Carmen and Tony.

Emilio Urberuaga

Gilda the Giant Sheep was published in Europe 25 years ago.

The author, Emilio Urberuaga, has won the National Prize for Illustration in Spain and is one of the most highly-regarded illustrators in Europe.

On the 25th anniversary of its release, *Gilda the Giant Sheep* is being published for the first time in English. For this edition, all the illustrations have been redone by the author, keeping in mind the originals. The text has also been reviewed following the original story.

Gilda the Giant Sheep
Somos8 Series

© Text and illustrations: Emilio Urberuaga, 1993/2018
© Edition: NubeOcho, 2018
www.nubeocho.com – hello@nubeocho.com

Original title: *Gilda, la oveja gigante*
English translation: Ben Dawlatly
Text editing: Rebecca Packard

Distributed in the United States by
Consortium Book Sales & Distribution

First edition in this series: 2018
ISBN: 978-84-17123-24-6

Printed in China by Asia Pacific Offset,
respecting international labor standards.

GILDA

the Giant Sheep

Emilio Urberuaga

There was once
a giant sheep named
Gilda.

The twenty shepherds that lived with her were
in charge of shearing her to sell the wool and
milking her to sell the milk and make cheese.

All that work was very tiring. One night, they
all got together to find a solution because they
didn't want to work anymore.

One shepherd had an idea:

"Why don't we chop Gilda up and sell the meat at the market? She's so big that we'd make a lot of money."

All the shepherds agreed.

"How nasty those shepherds are!" thought Gilda as she was running. "I never kicked them while they were milking me and I let them shear me without saying *baa* even when they nipped me with the shears."

"And now they want to turn me into mutton stew! Is it too much to ask for a sheep to grow old in peace?"

While Gilda was mulling things over, she arrived in a place full of tall buildings. It was early morning and there were people everywhere.

Gilda was so frightened by all the cars and
all the people that she climbed right up to
the top of a building. She looked like a huge
woolly cloud.

As she scoped the area for a meadow, her eyes
settled on an enormous, colorful piece of fabric.
Perhaps she could rest there?

When she got closer, she started to see animals.
Some small, others a little bigger, and some
locked in cages. All the animals looked very sad.

"Good morning," said Gilda politely.

"Can I help you?" asked the circus manager indifferently.

"I'm looking for somewhere to stay."

"And what can you do? Can you dance? Can you swing on the trapeze?"

"Oh, no, no… I can provide milk and wool."

"That's no good for a circus. Stop wasting my time."

Gilda left the circus very sad.
"I'm completely useless," she thought.
"Nobody loves me."

She was walking, lost in her thoughts,
when suddenly she heard a cry for help.

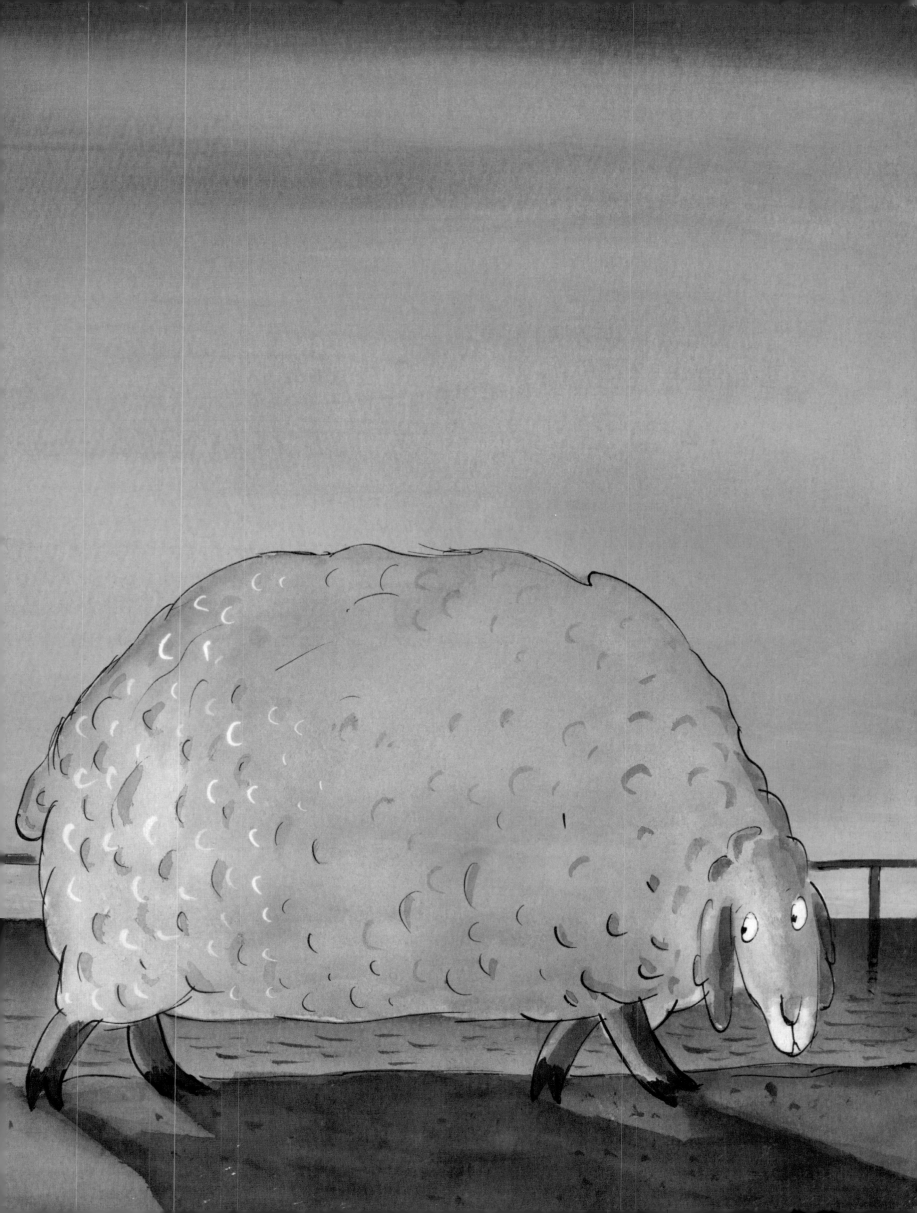

Gilda was very scared of water, but she jumped in to save the little sheep without giving it a second thought.

"Thank you! I was running away from the wolves when I fell into the water, and I can't swim."

"What are wolves?" asked Gilda.

"Don't you know what they are? Maybe you've never seen them because you're so big that they're scared of you… Do you know what? It would be amazing if you came with me and helped me and my flock with the wolves."

And together they climbed the hill where the little sheep lived.

When the wolves saw such a giant
sheep, they ran away terrified!

Gilda stayed to live with her new friends.

"I've never seen anything so big, so white and so beautiful," sighed Gilda.

"I certainly have!" replied her little friend.

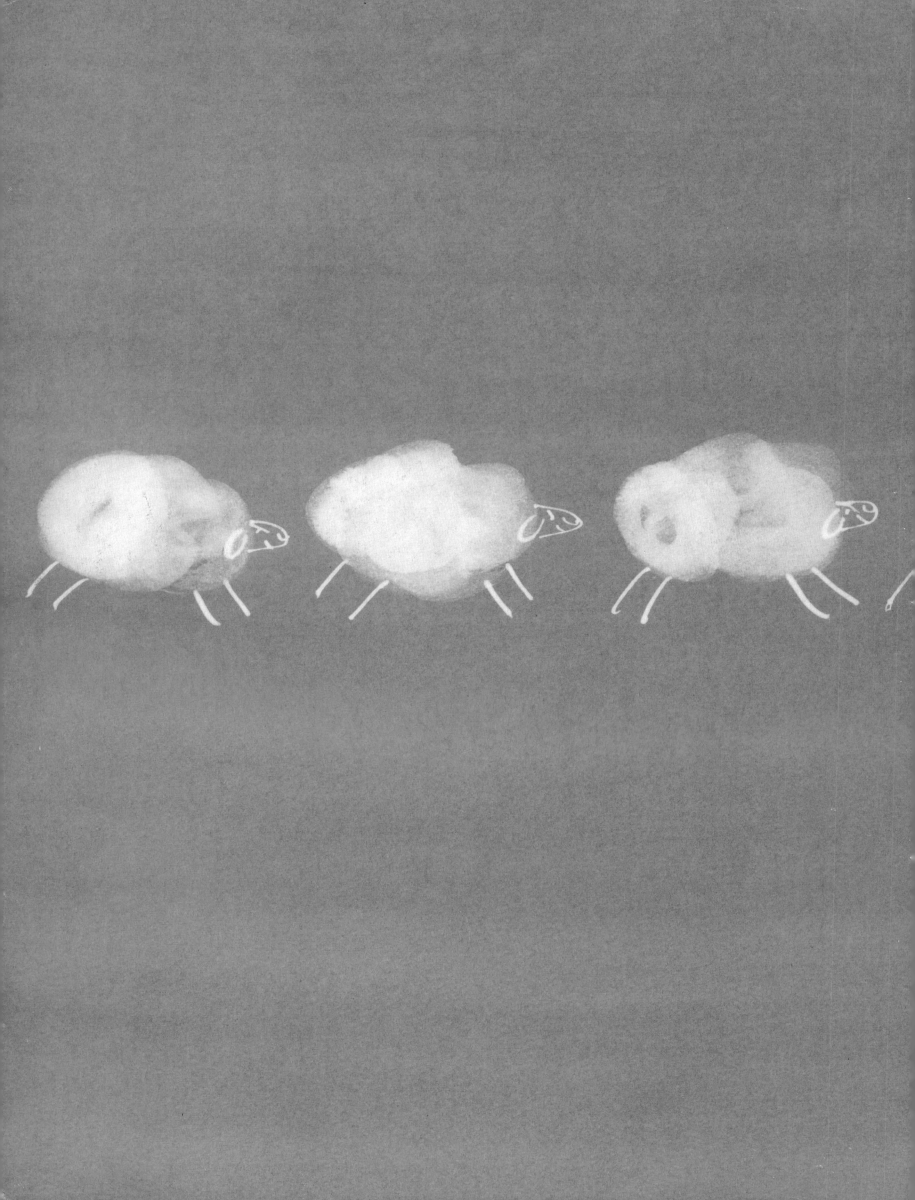